MW01170799

Dead Reckoning

By

MJ Allaire

Bookateer Publishing
www.bookateerpublishing.com

Layout and design by Ryan Twomey
Cover Images courtesy of Shutterstock

ISBN: 978-1-936476-05-3
Library of Congress Control Number: 2012915848

Bookateer Publishing
Box 5
Uncasville, CT 06382
www.bookateerpublishing.com

Death is a debt to nature due,
Which I have paid and so must you.

- Anonymous epitaph

Dedication

To Ryan, the wonderful man who will be my husband in a few short weeks. Thank you for all your hard work and fantastic ideas. This one's for you, just like my heart.

Mrs. Harkins ~
This story is short, not-so-sweet, and has no dragons, but I think it's my best yet...
Enjoy!
MJ Allaire

Mrs. Hawkins ~

This story is short,
not-so-sweet, and yes,
on occasion, but I think
it's my best yet...
Enjoy! Blessings,
Jill Green

Llyssaer didn't like her life. She didn't like her school, where she lived, or most of the people in this oddball, loveless, rinky-dink town. Although she was a pretty girl, with wide blue eyes and silky hair the color of burnt sienna, it didn't seem to make a bit of difference to anyone around her what she looked like. If she'd had five arms and tentacles for hair she doubted they would give her more than a second glance. Even her parents seemed to barely notice her anymore. When was the last time the three of them had done anything together as a family? Most days her parents were so busy they hardly knew she was there, the neighbors turned their backs to her whenever she walked by their houses, and the kids at school…

She sighed. She didn't want to think about it. Not any of it.

Once, not so long ago, her life had been fairly idyllic for a teenager. An only child, she had loved school, had lots of friends, made good grades, and got along well with the neighbors, including the giant Saint Bernard, Princess, that *everyone* in the neighborhood seemed to hate.

Then, somehow, things changed.

She kicked a rock along the now familiar cobblestone trail she followed on her way to school five days a week as memories of times past floated through her mind. The jagged piece of hardened earth offered no resistance to her shoe and tumbled to the side of the path. When it eventually plopped into a leaf-filled, mucky puddle, she barely noticed the muffled splash it made. Although her eyes stared at the trail ahead of her in the distance, her memories carried her back to happier times – back to a place in her life before her world had turned completely upside down.

It seemed as though a whisper of time had passed since she was living with her parents in their two-story gabled cape home in Connecticut. Her father was in the Navy and frequently traveled to distant places engaging in secret missions on his submarine. As a result, Llyssaer and her mother were left to run the household.

Her mother had been a housewife during Llyssaer's first few years in school but had since gone back to work. At the time it was all well and good, but eventually Llyssaer realized she was spending more time alone than she would have ever imagined possible. Solitude suited her just fine, though; she may have enjoyed spending time with her friends and family, but she didn't mind being alone.

She had been a good girl back then; well, for the most part. So much so that some of the kids in school referred to her as "that stick in the mud." And maybe, in a way, they were right, but it wasn't like she was trying to be that proverbial *stick* on purpose. She'd heard horror stories about kids doing bad things and, a few years ago, she had just decided she didn't want to be one of them. She always tried to do the right thing and be the best she could in anything she did. Did that make her a stick in the mud? Maybe, but if it did then so be it.

Sure, she'd had lots of friends when she'd lived in the Nutmeg State, but she'd been one of the lucky ones who hadn't gotten into a lot of mischief, much to the chagrin of many of those same friends. She supposed her parents could be thanked for this. Although her father had been away frequently with his job in the military, there was no doubt that she had been Daddy's little girl.

At a very early age, he had begun calling her Llys, which was convenient for those who had a problem pronouncing her given name. Her family and close friends all called her by this pet name, unless she was in trouble, of course, and she couldn't deny that she always wanted to be the apple of her father's eye. Since she was very close to him she knew that if she got into trouble while he was gone, his disappointment in her would be oh so much worse than any discipline which might happen as a consequence of her actions.

Llyssaer took a large bite of her Granny Smith apple and looked at her watch, 7:10 a.m. She had to be at school by 7:30 and still had roughly a half a mile to go. She would make it in time and be there early to boot.

"Joy," she mumbled with sarcasm.

With the final bite of her apple, she tossed it into the nearby bushes. She normally wasn't one to litter, but this was nature going back to nature, so it was okay, wasn't it?

From the corner of Llyssaer's eye, a faint glimpse of something caught her attention. She turned to look in the direction where she'd seen the movement and, at first, didn't see anything, but after a few seconds she noticed a girl close to her own age standing partially hidden by a tree off to Llyssaer's left. Beyond this nameless stranger was a small field filled with dry grass and scattered weeds. The girl, whoever she might be, was watching her.

Llyssaer stopped and returned the watcher's gaze, a little surprised to see her but not really scared. Being an only child, Llyssaer was a tomboy through and through and had every confidence she could put the spying female to the ground if she needed to. Either that or she would just slug her over the head with her backpack. The two inch thick math book she carried within the coarse, black fabric holstered across her back could knock out a muscular, fully grown man if she hit him with it; of that she was certain.

The girl watched her for several long seconds but made no move to approach. Her hair hung past her shoulders, blonde and curly. Although Llyssaer couldn't see her observer's eyes, she felt this uncanny prescience that hidden underneath were peering orbs of soft, sea green or maybe a speckled shade of gray. She gave the girl a slight nod to acknowledge her presence then turned and continued on her way. Llyssaer had no doubt if she was late for school, Mom would have her head.

She could have taken the bus to and from school like all the other kids in town but she chose not to, which was no easy accomplishment. Her mother was old fashioned, believing that a teenage girl with no older brothers to protect her would be inviting trouble if she walked back and forth to school by herself every day. In spite of this, Llyssaer had been adamant when citing her reasons for wanting to walk.

"Obesity in this country is rapidly going out of control, mostly because people are lazy.

I don't want to be one of them!"

"The daily walk will give me great exercise," she insisted, *"and the fresh air and sunshine are a bonus!"*

She also argued that she was fifteen now… *FIFTEEN*… and although she knew her mother loved her very much, she couldn't protect Llyssaer from everything. When would her mother let her spread her wings and fly? When she was 40?

Another reason, which she hadn't told her mother, was simply that the kids on the bus didn't like her. Heck, as far as she could tell, the kids in the entire school didn't like her. Being the new girl in a new school in a new town, she was surprised they never bullied her like some kids did when new students breached their familiar atmosphere. But even without any bullying she still sensed she didn't fit in. Sometimes, it was in the looks they gave her and sometimes in the looks they didn't. When walking through the hallway she might pass a group of chattering schoolmates and as she approached a strange silence would fall over them like a thick blanket of quiet. Once in a while she would hear the buzz of whispering behind her back after she had passed, but most of the time she never heard anything from them at all. It was almost as if she didn't exist.

The kids in this town were strange and she longed for her old town, her old home, her old school, her old friends. Why did they have to leave?

She sighed. She knew why, her parents had explained it to her, but she doubted they told her everything. Parents almost never tell you *everything*.

Llyssaer swung her gaze around to see if the peeping female was following her, but the path behind her was now empty. She wondered, absently, where the curious blonde waif might have gone but soon her mental focus returned back to her parents and how she had ended up here.

After spending quite a few years as a housewife raising Llyssaer, her mother Pauline had finally decided she was ready for something more from life. She began writing short stories as a way to occupy her time and eventually found her calling as a full time author. As Llyssaer approached those tender teenage years, with a mother who travelled frequently to promote her books and a father devoted to the military, Llyssaer found herself surprisingly independent. Although she would sometimes stay with friends or family while her parents were gone at the same time, Llyssaer embraced the idea of raising herself. Her cousin Daniel lived in the next town, which was perfect on a weekend, but during the week it ended up being too much of a hassle to cart her back and forth so she could catch the bus for school. After all, he had his own family and children to raise.

Realizing their situation was changing, Llyssaer's parents enlisted the help of their neighbor next door, Mrs. Grenadine, or Mrs. Gren as Llyssaer liked to call her.

A gray-eyed single woman in her mid-50s, Mrs. Gren was a widow and lived alone. She could frequently be seen in her yard gardening, mowing, or hanging out the laundry. Her short, neatly cropped hair had begun graying long ago, but every time Llyssaer saw her bustling around her yard in the sun, she couldn't help but notice some of the blonde highlights of youth mixed in with her neat, gray mane of age as it struggled for dominance atop the older woman's head.

Mrs. Gren was a supporter of the red, white and blue through and through and since she knew that Llyssaer's father, Andy, was frequently away on deployments, she was always checking in on Llys and her mother. Mrs. Gren lovingly referred to them as "the girls next door." When she learned of their predicament surrounding the times when both Llyssaer's mother and father would be away on travel, Mrs. Gren generously volunteered to keep a close eye on the teenage girl.

With one less obstacle on their plate and realizing their travel schedules might overlap more often than they liked, Andy and Pauline decided to get Llyssaer a dog, both for companionship as well as protection. The dog, a German Shepherd aptly named Jiminy Cricket, or Crick-a-tick for short, proved to be worth his weight in gold.

With mostly black on top, soft shades of brown beneath, and a bushy, black tail, Crick-a-tick followed Llyssaer around everywhere. The canine companion watched over Llys like his namesake character from *Pinocchio*, a story the girl had loved as a child. For a while when he was a puppy, she actually reconfigured one of her cloth backpacks so she could carry the pooch around on her back. With her backpack straps pulled as tight as they would go, she loved walking around the house and neighborhood with her curious companion looking over her shoulder like the famed cartoon cricket. Before long, however, the furry beast outgrew the backpack and was soon traipsing around alongside his mistress, day in and day out.

Since Llyssaer spent time with Mrs. Gren at least a few days a week it was only natural that Crick-a-tick, soon shortened to simply Crick, would form a bond with the gray-haired woman as well. Llys used to joke with Mrs. Gren that Crick's main reason for accompanying her to the house next door was because of the leftover steak bones he received from the older woman on occasion, but in her heart she had no doubt that her special bundle of fur loved the grandmotherly woman just as much as she did.

Llyssaer had just turned twelve when they brought Crick-a-tick into their home and was nearly fifteen when she'd lost him. The unfortunate, horrific event surrounding this loss is what marked the beginning of the end of her happy, idyllic life.

*****

During recent years, crime across the United States had become rampant and Connecticut offered no safe haven from the storm. When two men carried out a home invasion on the western side of the Nutmeg State, killing nearly everyone who lived there, their crime made national news. A few months prior to this incident, however, there had been another home invasion on the eastern side of the state which didn't receive nearly as much media attention, but should have.

This was the day Llyssaer's life changed forever.

The single event which so drastically transformed Llyssaer's world as she knew it occurred the previous year at the tail end of a remarkably mild winter. There had been an increased number of break-ins around the town where she lived since the New Year, and residents of the Nutmeg State were on edge. Llyssaer's parents warned her to be home before dark, at least until the days got longer, which generally meant she had very little time outside at all once she got home from school and finished her chores. It seemed totally unreasonable to her that, during those long, dreary winter months in New England, nature chose to have daylight disappear well before dinner was ready. Understanding her parents' concern, however, Llyssaer did her best to be home to do her homework long before the sun went down.

On this particular day, which would be infinitely burned into her memory, Llyssaer had come home from school to an empty house, gathered up Crick-a-tick, and gone next door. After chatting with Mrs. Gren over a few freshly baked chocolate chip cookies and a tall glass of milk, Llyssaer had returned home around 5:00 p.m. Her father was on a deployment and her mother had been in an all-day meeting in Hartford but had gotten stuck in traffic on her way home. In spite of this, Llyssaer decided to take Crick-a-tick home and start dinner so a meal would be on the table, or close to it, by the time her mother arrived.

After getting Crick settled and locking the doors, Llyssaer grabbed the recipe she'd printed from a website earlier that day and set to work. Two cans of tuna, two cans of cream of mushroom soup, a couple cups of baby peas, a bag of egg noodles, some milk and a fresh tube of Ritz crackers… the main ingredients for a rockin' tuna casserole.

It had been a year since the event that had so dramatically changed her life but memories held her to that fateful afternoon like barnacles to a ship's hull.

She plugged her earphones into her ears and listened to Chris Cagle's crooning voice while she prepared the meal. She took her time, cleaning up her mess as she made it, then popped the prepared dish into the oven to bake. Her mother texted her saying she would be home around 6:00 p.m. It was almost 5:45 p.m. and cook time would be about 25 minutes. It would be close, but this way her mother could have a few minutes to relax and they could chit-chat while the meal rested before they began their feast.

As the aroma of baking tuna filtered through the kitchen, Llyssaer sat at the table with her math book spread open to her left and her notebook to her right, working on that night's homework. Although she'd turned the music from the iPod down to a more reasonable level, she still listened to it as she worked on one problem after the next.

She smiled and reached down to pet Crick-a-tick, who was almost always by her side, but all she felt was air. She leaned to the side to see if he was lying under the table, but he wasn't.

"Crick! Where did you wander off to?" she called out in a teasing tone as her gaze moved across the room to the dog's food and water bowls. She knew the water dish was full and fresh because she had just changed it before she started dinner. The food dish was nearly full with kibble but it looked as though he had been snacking while she was cooking because there was a slight crater smack dab in the middle of the pile of food. The German Shepherd, however, was nowhere to be seen.

She pulled the ear bud out of her left ear and listened. Where was he hiding?

"Crick?"

With Sir Cagle still crooning away on the right side of her head, Llyssaer thought she heard something but couldn't make out what it was. She pushed the stop button on her iPod and removed the other ear plug then listened again. At first the only sound she detected was silence, but within seconds she heard a distinctive scratching noise coming from one of the darkened rooms somewhere down the hallway.

"Crick?" she called again, but the dog remained unseen.

Feeling the unwelcomed sensation of butterflies swirling like a tornado in the pit of her stomach, Llyssaer set her iPod down on top of her math book and pushed her chair away from the table. The noise she'd heard sounded like it had come from the back bedroom but she couldn't imagine what Crick might be scratching at in there. Did he hear a chipmunk in the walls?

She began making her way down the hallway to investigate but just as she passed the oven, the buzzer bleated and made her jump. The casserole was done.

Frowning at the inconvenient act of having to deal with dinner when her mind was elsewhere, Llyssaer stepped over to the counter, quickly grabbed a pair of hot mitts from where they hung on the wall, and removed the casserole from the oven. She had just set the prepared meal on the stovetop when she heard the scratching sound again. This time it was accompanied with a long, low whine.

"Cricket? What's wrong, buddy? Come here, boy!"

Instead of coming to her like he usually did, the Shepherd whined again from the back bedroom. Something wasn't right.

Llyssaer began making her way down the hallway toward her parents' bedroom when she realized she didn't have any kind of weapon for self-defense. What if someone had gotten into the house and she hadn't heard a thing? She had been listening to her iPod, after all, and probably too loud. She smiled as she thought of her mother's constant nagging about the volume level Llys liked, then shuddered as another thought immediately filled her mind... what if Crick-a-tick was lying on the floor in the back room, battered and bloody after finding the intruder?

"No," she said firmly as she shook her head in denial. Her mind was spooking her and she refused to think anything like that could happen, not in this neighborhood. Their house was secure and Crick was a good watch dog.

In spite of her attempt at self-reassurance, Llyssaer quickly walked back to the living room and grabbed the poker leaning against the fireplace mantle. It might not be a great weapon but at least it was something. It wasn't like she could gouge an intruder to death with her neat, although very short, fingernails.

Without a word, she crept back down the hall and made her way toward the rear bedroom, thinking about her options. It didn't take long for her to decide she would curl her hand around the door frame to turn on the bedroom light then jump back so she could survey the illuminated room.

Before she did anything, she paused and listened; the house was silent. She took a deep breath and reached for the door frame. Just as her hand began its quest for the light switch on the other side, a sudden blur of dark color rushed through the doorway, brushed against her legs, and scurried back down the hall toward the kitchen. If she hadn't been so startled with the unexpected flurry of motion, she might have had time to swing the poker held tightly in her hand at the unidentified shape as it flew by.

Turning to look after the unidentified shape, she realized it was a good thing she hadn't reacted like she probably should have. Crick-a-tick had reached the kitchen door and was now barking furiously at it, begging to be let outside.

"My God, Crick! You scared the crap out of me!" she scolded but he paid her no mind. As if in response to her outburst, he was now jumping up at the door, still barking like a mad dog.

Llyssaer caught a sudden image in her head of the canine from the movie *Cujo* and chuckled. Crick was too lovable to be anything at all like that mutt from the book written by Stephen King, one of her favorite authors. Although she was glad to see Crick wasn't a drooling, evil bundle of fur, a knot of fear still formed in her chest as she stood in the hallway staring at her muscular, but usually very friendly, companion. She'd had him since he was eight weeks old – a beautiful, innocently round bundle of joy – and during the past two years, she'd never seen him act like this. What had gotten into him?

"Crick!" she yelled, her voice stern and unwavering. She lowered the poker to the floor but did not set it down. "Come here!"

She tapped her makeshift weapon on the hardwood floor as she emphasized the end of her command, but instead of following her order, the dog stopped jumping and sat down on the mat just in front of the door. His haunches twitched with anxiety and he stared at her with wide, agitated eyes. He barked three times then whined a long, low cry that slowly turned into a growl as he turned and pushed his nose into the crack of the door.

It was obvious to Llys that he wanted her to open it, but she'd never seen him like this before. She contemplated whether or not she should let him out and had finally decided to go get his leash when the door handle jiggled and the lock rotated one quarter of a turn then rotated completely as it was opened from the outside. Before her mind understood what was happening, the door swung inward with a gentle swish.

"No!" Llyssaer cried as her mother pushed the door open more than enough for the dog's sleek, slender body to get through. Without waiting for a leash, Crick-a-tick darted past Pauline and disappeared into the darkness beyond.

"Oh!" Llyssaer's mother cried as she stumbled backwards. In his haste to go out, their four-legged family member nearly knocked her over. Thankfully, she'd been able to grab one of the railings that framed each side of the stairs on the tiny porch.

"Llys?" Pauline asked as she stared at her daughter, her eyes piercing and full of questions. "What's going on?"

Llyssaer dropped the poker and it fell to the floor with a bouncing thump. Her eyes widened with shock and confusion as she brushed past her mother and lunged into the darkness in pursuit of her beloved pet.

"It's Crick! Something's wrong!" the girl explained as she followed the dog.

"Llys, stop!" her mother ordered.

Pauline dropped her purse on the kitchen table then quickly made her way over to the refrigerator. She grabbed two of the half dozen flashlights stored there then turned back to the doorway and handed one to her impatiently waiting daughter. Llyssaer was bouncing from foot to foot now, anxious to go after her furry friend.

"I don't know what he's doing, but he was whining and barking like crazy..." the girl tried to explain.

"It's okay," her mother said. "Go! Let's find him!"

Side by side and with a pair of glowing beacons lighting their way, the miniature search party ran into the darkness in pursuit of the barking dog.

The rocky, leaf-littered path Llyssaer had been walking on dumped her out of the cover of the woods and onto the shoulder of a two-lane, blacktop road. Before she reached the paved area, she turned left and headed toward the brick, three-story building she saw in the distance. As she made her way toward the school, a long, yellow school bus passed by on her right, moving in the same direction. She watched as its left turn signal began to blink erratically when the ancient, multi-windowed beast prepared to turn into the main parking lot. In less than thirty seconds, it would do its very best impersonation of an extended, discolored clown car, releasing all of its occupants before the front door of the circus known as school.

Remembering the girl she'd seen in the woods, Llyssaer turned and glanced over her shoulder again. No one was following her. She wondered where the girl had gone and who she might be. Although Llyssaer had only been a member of this school for a few weeks, she didn't think she'd ever seen the girl here before. But then again, how much had she really paid attention to any particular individual? Not much.

When she finally reached the parking lot, Llyssaer weaved through the rows of empty cars and walked toward the main entrance. As she approached the double doors leading to the foyer, she passed a group of girls who were chatting excitedly and tossing their hair over their shoulders like models. Although they never looked her in the eye, it was obvious they knew she was passing by because their conversation ebbed into silence.

Cheerleaders – the future of America, Llys thought sarcastically without giving them a second glance. She ignored the cluster of young women and stepped through one of the propped open, glass doors then made her way into the main foyer. She maneuvered carefully through the throng of mingling teens and finally found her way to the cafeteria. There, she skirted a cluster of tables until she reached the row of vending machines on the far wall. Finding the one she was looking for, she pushed her hand into her pants pocket until her fingers found the smooth, cool pile of coins buried there.

What should I have today? she thought. As if in answer, her stomach grumbled while she surveyed the contents.

The shelves of the automated machine were fairly full and she had numerous choices. Along the top few rows, her eyes surveyed things such as granola bars, pop tarts, and crackers with cheese. Crammed into specially-sized slots through the middle rows were candy bars like Snickers, Hersheys and Mr. Goodbar. Neatly aligned along the shelves in the bottom third of the machine were healthier choices such as instant oatmeal in a microwave safe tub, yogurt and fruit. She eyed the blueberry pop tarts on the topmost shelf for several long seconds but eventually decided on a healthier start to her day. God knew she would need it. Her earlier apple had been small and definitely couldn't be considered any sort of a meal.

She dropped the exact change into the coin slot of the machine and watched as a medium-sized container of strawberry yogurt and a small box of sweet golden raisins dropped into the bin at the bottom with a soft *thunk*.

The breakfast of champions, she thought as she glanced at her watch. The first bell would ring any second now. Luckily her first class was only two doors away from the cafeteria. This would give her five minutes to eat. She had plenty of time.

With her backpack still strapped snugly across her back, she leaned against the sill of the nearby window and stared outside while she consumed the yogurt and raisin combination. About two dozen students littered the tables on the other side of the cafeteria, making it difficult for her to hear their jumbled conversations, but she didn't care. Instead, her thoughts drifted back to the girl in the woods.

Who was she and what had she been doing there? Did she go to this school? What grade was she in? What was her name?

The crash of a lunch chair falling over backwards startled Llyssaer and she turned around to see what happened. Mike, a dark-haired boy in her English class, was playfully wrestling with another boy she did not recognize. Their antics had knocked the chair over next to the group of students at the far end of the room.

A few tables away, one of the cafeteria monitors, Mr. Keegan or Kardin or something similar, held a hand out toward the boys.

"Okay guys, let's move along and find our way to class."

The boys looked over at the man, grabbed their bags reluctantly then headed for the door. Before they got there, the monitor cleared his throat and pointed at the chair, still lying on its back where it had landed next to the table.

"The chair?" he asked expectantly.

"I'll get it," the boy with no name said as he turned back to the table. Without another word he stood the chair up, pushed it under the table, and followed Mike to the cafeteria door.

"Thank you, young man," Mr. Keegan/Kardin said as his eyes surveyed the lunch room. When he spotted Llyssaer standing at the window, he looked at her wordlessly and raised an eyebrow.

"I'm almost finished," Llyssaer offered in response to his unanswered question then scraped the bottom of her yogurt container with her plastic utensil. "Just a few more bites."

The man nodded silently and turned to make his way toward a small group of whispering students at the other end of the cafeteria. As he did, the first bell rang.

Llyssaer returned her gaze back to the scenery outside the cafeteria window and chuckled. It didn't take long for her eyes to focus on a sparkling, dew-covered leaf just as movement next to a thick line of bushes caught her attention. At first she thought it was nothing, a bird maybe, but after just a second or two, she realized what she was seeing.

It was the girl from the woods.

Llyssaer watched as the young, blonde female peeked around the bushes then turned her attention to the cafeteria window. They stared at each other for what felt like an eternity when the unnamed girl finally offered a timid wave of friendship. Llyssaer, with her yogurt cup in one hand and spoon in the other, wiggled the plastic, cream smeared utensil back at the stranger in silent reply.

Remembering the first bell had already rang, she turned and glanced at the clock on the wall; she would have to get going soon or she would be late to class.

Llyssaer scooped the last bit of yogurt and raisins into her mouth and cautiously peered over her shoulder at the cafeteria monitor. He was talking to the woman cashier now, his back to the window. Llys tossed her yogurt container and spoon into the nearby garbage can and stole one more glance outside. The blonde girl was still partially hidden by the bushes, watching her. Llyssaer offered her an awkward, yet friendly, smile and tapped at her watch, then pointed toward the cafeteria door. In response, the girl shook her head and gestured for Llyssaer to come outside.

Come outside? She only had a few minutes until the last bell rang. If she got to class after it did she would be marked tardy. She'd only been in this school for a few weeks and had already been close to being late a couple of times. There was no doubt that if she actually didn't make it to class on time, or, heaven forbid, decided to *skip* a class, her mother would most certainly find out about it. With everything else they'd been through over the past few months, Llyssaer really didn't want to invite that kind of trouble. She was having a hard enough time adjusting to her new life as it was.

But then again, first period today would be English, and they would only be discussing the essays they'd written last week. She thought she'd done well on hers, but had no idea what grade she had gotten. Today they would get back the graded papers and talk about them. Ugh.

She looked at her watch again – the final bell would ring in just over a minute if the time on her purple and lavender Timex was accurate. Turning to look out the window one more time, Llyssaer saw that the girl was still there, in the same place, gesturing for her to come outside.

Llyssaer's curiosity regarding the stranger got the better of her. Her hunger to know who this girl was and what she had been doing in the woods earlier was stronger than her desire to know what grade she'd gotten on her essay. She could find that out tomorrow. And as far as her mother was concerned… well, if her mother found out she'd been late to class, Llyssaer would just have to make her understand.

Somehow.

Raising an index finger in a "wait" gesture, Llyssaer turned and walked hastily out of the cafeteria, surprised to see the hall beyond the doors now empty. She turned and headed toward the main entrance but hesitated when she realized she might be better off going down the hall a short distance and exiting through the side door instead. If anyone stopped her she would simply explain that she'd dropped her pen outside and was going to retrieve it.

Wearing a gray t-shirt, blue jeans, and black sneakers, her rubber-soled footsteps were barely audible as she hurried to the side door through the still empty passageway. After a few seconds, she thought she might actually make it outside without encountering a single person when she heard the unmistakable sound of someone walking somewhere behind her. She glanced back nervously, wondering who it was, and sighed with relief when she saw Joe, one of the Johnson twins, as he passed through the intersection of the hallways. She sighed with relief again when he disappeared, having never looked in her direction.

This is too easy, she thought. *No one ever notices me anyways, so it's not like it's a big deal.*

As the final bell echoed through the inner hallways of the school, Llyssaer stepped through the thick, steel door and out into the bright, morning sunshine.

Thankfully there was no one outside, just as she'd hoped. Llyssaer turned left and made her way toward the side of the school where she'd seen the young girl through the cafeteria window – one more corner to go.

The morning dew on the grass dampened the toes of her shoes and she frowned when she felt the moisture soaking into the tips of her socks. If there was one thing she absolutely detested, it was wearing wet socks. In Connecticut, never knowing what to expect from the beautiful, yet totally unpredictable, New England weather, she'd almost always kept an extra pair of dry socks in her backpack. Since moving to a warmer climate, however, she hadn't even considered it. She hadn't thought she needed to.

"Bah," she whispered, resolving to put a pair of socks in her backpack when she got home later on. After today she wouldn't be stuck wearing wet socks again, not if she could help it.

She approached the final corner of the building and stopped abruptly, frowning as she looked down at her shoes. They were now wet from toe to mid foot. It was going to be one of those days.

Just as she was about to start walking again, the shadow of an approaching, unidentified figure appeared on the grass at the corner of the building. Startled, Llyssaer prepared to use her lost pen excuse when she discovered she wouldn't need to. It was the mysterious blonde girl.

"Hi," the girl greeted nervously.

"Hi," Llyssaer said with a shy smile. "I can't stay long; I'm going to be late for class. Did you need something?"

The tow-headed girl stared at the ground shyly for several seconds before she finally turned to look up at Llyssaer.

"Do you like dogs?" she blurted

out, her voice low and trembling with uncertainty.

"Me?" Llyssaer asked in surprise as she pointed at her own chest.

The girl nodded. "You look like someone who likes dogs."

A vision of Crick-a-tick suddenly filled Llyssaer's mind – his pointy ears, moist, black snout, and love-filled big brown eyes. Damn, she missed him! She felt tears stinging her eyes as she nodded. When she finally spoke, her voice was barely audible.

"I do."

"Mmm," the girl agreed with a nod. "Do you have any?"

Llyssaer quickly shook her head no and said in a sad whisper, "I did, but he died."

"Mmm," the girl said again. "Come with me. I have something to show you."

Llyssaer shook her head. "I can't. I have class."

The girl moved her own head in a similar fashion. "No. You really should follow me."

"Why?" Llyssaer asked as she shifted her backpack and glanced at her watch again. "And what's your name?"

The girl hesitated several seconds

before she answered. Then, with a sigh, she offered a single sentence that made Llyssaer's decision for her.

"My name is Joy and Jiminy wants you to follow me."

Jiminy.

Hearing her dog's real first name fall from the lips of this young female stranger brought Llyssaer back to the last night she'd seen her canine friend. Had it only been six months?

Her heart screamed, "No! Don't go there again! Not yet! It hurts too much!" At the same time, as if in a parallel world, her mind cried, "Go! Go with her! Look beyond the pain and maybe, just maybe, you can see him one more time!"

Llyssaer didn't hesitate. Since meeting the girl, she had not spoken her dog's name out loud, not even once, yet Joy somehow seemed to know him. But how could that be? How did she know Crick? Llyssaer had never known anyone named Joy in her life, nor had she been aware of any friends with a friend named Joy. Besides this, when she'd had Crick-a-tick in her life she'd lived in an entirely different state, away from this place and time, the people, and everything else she'd come to know over the past several months.

"What do you know about Crick?" Llyssaer asked Joy, but the girl had turned and was moving quickly toward the wooded area behind the school. It was almost as though she hadn't heard the question.

"Joy?" Llyssaer called out as she followed the blonde girl with slow uncertainty. "What do you know about my dog?"

Joy stopped and turned to look back at her.

"Please, just follow me, Llyssaer," Joy said quietly. "I can't tell you because you wouldn't understand. I have to show you."

With barely a glance back toward the large, three-story building where she was supposed to spend her day, Llyssaer followed the girl to the edge of the school grounds. When they reached the tree line, Joy stepped into the cool shadows and turned to make sure Llyssaer was following her.

"You need to see what I'm going to show you," Joy said as she held a branch out of the way for the dark-haired girl. "It's a special place not seen by many people. Jiminy needs you to see it, too."

"But how do you know him?" Llyssaer asked with a frown as she stepped beyond the branch and waited for Joy to lead the way.

"I can't explain it with words. Not yet, but once we get to the place I need to show you I promise I'll explain everything," the blonde stranger said quietly.

Wanting more information but realizing she would just have to be patient, Llyssaer stepped over a long forgotten log from a felled tree and glanced at her watch again. It was almost 7:45 a.m. If they got wherever they were going and saw whatever it was Joy wanted to show her, Llyssaer thought she might be able to get back to school pretty quickly. She would just have to think of some excuse to explain why she was late to class.

What would she tell them? If push

came to shove, quite a few people had seen her in the cafeteria, so it wasn't like she could say she'd overslept. Maybe she could use the excuse, "My friend, Bloody Mary, came for an unexpected, early visit and I didn't have the necessary items to deal with it." She sighed, certain that the school officials would then question her about why she hadn't just gone to the nurse for those necessary items. Following Joy as she led the way through a winding maze of crunching leaves and twigs, Llyssaer realized she may just have to fess up and admit she'd skipped her first class.

Oh, her mother would be furious, but Llyssaer would just have to worry about that later. Jiminy, and his memory, had taken precedence on that good old ladder of priorities.

Even though there hadn't been a cloud in the sky when Llyssaer arrived at school, she was surprised when she saw that the area around them had taken on a dismal, lackluster hue. In fact, the entire wooded area they were in had become downright dreary. Glancing into the trees ahead she was surprised to see a wide blanket of fog hovering from just above the ground to several feet in the air.

"Joy, are you sure you know where you're going?" Llyssaer whispered nervously, slowing with hesitation when she understood that the blonde girl was heading straight for the thickest part of the fog bank hovering in the distance.

"Yes, I do. It looks a bit… scary here, I know, but it gets better once we get past those trees," Joy answered as she pointed at the thickest part of the swirling white mist. Llyssaer stopped and stared at the tall stand of trees reaching for the sky through the wide, ivory blanket.

Joy stopped also and frowned at her. With a chuckle, she turned back and was soon standing two feet in front of the girl with the backpack.

"Come on," Joy encouraged. "You don't need to be scared. I know where I'm going. Honest I do."

Noticing the uncertainty covering Llyssaer's smooth face, the blonde girl added, "Do you want to hold my hand?"

Llyssaer's gaze was locked on the fog bank before them. She could feel the chilly air ahead, beckoning her forward into the dense, white cloud with cool, invisible fingers.

"Llyssaer," Joy said as she laid her

hand on her new friend's arm. Although the day was very warm, Llyssaer's skin was sprinkled with goose flesh and she jumped at the touch. "Do you want to hold my hand?"

Llyssaer turned to meet the blonde girl's eyes. They were an odd shade of gray with green flecks and for a long moment, she couldn't help but feel lost in them.

"Do you want to hold my hand? It's okay if you do…"

It was only when Joy repeated her question for a third time that Llyssaer finally found her voice to answer.

"No… no, I don't think I need to hold your hand." As if to emphasize her statement, she shook her head from side to side. "But if you don't mind, I think I would like to hold onto the back of your shirt. That fog looks pretty thick and I don't know the area like you do."

"Very well," Joy said. Without another word she turned her back toward her new friend until she faced the breathing band of moisture. She waited patiently for several seconds for Llyssaer to grab onto her pink shirt, which was littered with purple and yellow flowers. When Llyssaer finally had a good grip, Joy gave her a wordless nod and led them into the fog.

"Wait a second," Llyssaer said as a sudden thought struck her. She released Joy's top and stopped just a foot or so into the swirling mist as her blue eyes filled with doubt. After several long seconds, she took first one step, then another, away from the blonde stranger.

"Joy, how do you know my name?"

"I will explain it..." Joy began, but Llyssaer's nervous, questioning glance turned to anger as she stomped her foot into a pile of crunchy, brown leaves.

"No! I want you to tell me now! I want some answers right now, and if I don't get them I'm turning around and going back to the school!"

Joy shook her head as if in denial and looked calmly into the demanding, cobalt eyes staring back at her.

"I can't explain it here, Llys. You won't understand. Follow me just beyond those trees and I will tell you everything. There are things there that will..." She paused as she searched for the right words, "There are things there, and not here, that will help you understand."

Llyssaer stared at the fair-haired girl, her eyes still filled with doubt.

"I just don't feel comfortable not knowing…" she began, but Joy interrupted her in a soothing, almost adult-like voice.

"I know. All I can tell you is that Jiminy wants you to follow me. He's the one who told me your name. And if you follow me, you will understand. I promise."

Llyssaer's eyes filled with tears, her heart filled with emotion, her head filled with confusion.

"Jiminy?"

Joy nodded.

"I promise you I mean no harm, but I can offer you no more of an explanation. You must follow me if you want more, but if you must turn back, I understand."

Llyssaer wiped her eyes with the back of her hand, her entire being thoroughly engulfed with an array of conflicting emotions. She was incredibly nervous and uncomfortable by the unknown while an electric excitement coursed through her veins at the thought of Jiminy, her beloved canine friend, somehow communicating with this mysterious girl. Although her conscience told her she should go back to school and that being late was better than skipping the entire day, her desire to understand, to know more about the how and why this girl she'd just met knew anything about her beloved dog, overpowered everything else.

"Will you give me your word, your solemn word, that I can trust you?" Llyssaer asked the blonde girl in a quiet, uncertain voice.

"I do," Joy answered with a nod.

After several seconds of thought, Llyssaer finally spoke a single word and stepped forward.

"Okay."

Joy smiled and turned so Llyssaer could take hold of her shirt again then the girls slowly made their way into the heart of the ominous, milky bank of fog.

Llyssaer and her mother chased after Jiminy as his stream of melodic barks echoed, beckoning them through the cool, early evening air. They ran down their driveway and across the front yard before they realized where the muscular bundle of fur was heading; to the house next door.

The street light between their house and Mrs. Gren's had been out for the past few weeks, and oddly, their gray-haired neighbor hadn't turned on her porch light, either. As they approached the older woman's driveway, Pauline grabbed Llyssaer's arm, slowing her down.

"Wait," Pauline said quietly as she raised an index finger to her own ear. "Listen."

Llyssaer stopped and did as her mother suggested. Crick-a-tick's barks had changed from an echoed warning to alarmed growls.

"He's inside!" the girl cried. Without waiting for her mother's approval, Llyssaer darted up the driveway and into the dark house.

"No!" Pauline called after her daughter, but Llyssaer didn't hear her. Her mind was focused on the rumbling sound being created deep in Crick-a-tick's throat. It was an eerie, rare sound which overshadowed the weak moans coming from Mrs. Gren's living room.

Llyssaer stumbled up the twin steps leading into the neighbor's kitchen as her flashlight quickly panned across the room she'd been in not more than an hour ago. The familiar space was empty and not at all the way it was when she'd left. The table had been pushed up against the sink and two of the four chairs had been overturned and now lay on their sides. The trash can, normally directly below the oven on the far wall, had been knocked over and its spilled contents littered the floor around it.

Llyssaer turned her flashlight beam towards the living room. When it illuminated the tan carpet next to the couch, she noticed a trail of dark, reddish-brown splotches connecting the kitchen to the living room.

As if in a dream, she heard her mother's voice just beyond the kitchen door as she spoke frantically on her cell phone. It registered in Llyssaer's mind that her mother had called 911 and help would soon be on the way, but she couldn't wait. Crick needed her! And where was Mrs. Gren?

A moan beyond the couch blocked out her mother's voice and Llys took a careful step forward. Shining her light around the longest piece of furniture in the room, she barely recognized the bloody figure curled up on the floor.

Mrs. Gren's face was different, somehow distorted; it wasn't the face of the woman she knew, yet still, it was. She lay on her left side in a fetal position, rocking slightly. The only eye Llyssaer could see, her right one, was swollen almost to the size of a glossy, purple plum. As the woman rolled onto her back with a groan of discomfort, Llyssaer couldn't help but stare at her shirt. It was the same one she'd had on earlier. On the front was a still photo of Kenny Rogers, a microphone held to his mouth, frozen forever in the middle of a song. Mrs. Gren had just been telling Llyssaer earlier about how this particular t-shirt was one of her favorite things to wear, stressing that she only wore it when she was in a nostalgic mood. She boasted that some of her old concert t-shirts were worn and discolored now, but not this one! This one still looked almost brand new…

But it didn't anymore.

The front of Mrs. Gren's favorite t-shirt was now mostly covered with wide, dark streaks of blood. There was a ragged hole in the side and the ends were tattered in a few places as if they'd been ripped in a fit of anger.

Llyssaer looked back at Mrs. Gren's face again and froze in shock. At first she'd thought, in some far corner of her mind, perhaps the older woman had fallen in the dark and hit her face on the corner of the coffee table, but now she knew it was more serious. This definitely wasn't some simple injury that could be taken care of with a band aid, a kiss, and a chocolate chip cookie.

Oh, crapola! This woman I have come to love like a grandmother was beaten up and is lying on the ground right before me, she thought with shocked surprise.

When the older woman suddenly rolled onto her back, Llyssaer clearly saw much more carnage than she'd ever dreamed she could or would ever see, even in her worst nightmare.

Mrs. Gren's face, oh her poor face, had been transformed from that of an innocent, loving grandmother to a lumpy mass of distended flesh. Her bottom lip was bleeding and her left cheekbone was bruised and had swollen so much that it looked like a goose egg the size of Manhattan. The skin above her left eyebrow had been sliced open and blood was streaming down the side of her face, and her hair…

Normally combed and neat, every strand in place, her hair was now a mish-mashed mess and made her look as though she'd just woken up from a bad dream. The injured woman moaned again as she lifted a shaking hand and pointed a bloody finger towards the hallway.

"There," she whispered, her voice

trembling with pain. Llyssaer stared in disbelief as Mrs. Gren's blood-smeared arm fell to the carpet with a soft *thud*.

Suddenly, from somewhere down the hallway, Crick growled once, twice then barked frantically at something unseen. Llyssaer's heart was torn with uncertainty as she struggled to decide what to do.

Mrs. Gren moaned again as Crick's yelps of alarm ended with an unexpected abruptness and she immediately shifted the beam of her flashlight from the battered woman on the floor to the hallway, her heart frozen with terror. Another loud bark of pain followed by a single, high-pitched whimper pierced the air for half a second before silence surrounded them as if they'd been sequestered in a sound-proof room. Torn between staying with the injured woman on the living room floor or saving her dog, Llyssaer hesitated. The damage to Mrs. Gren was already done and her mother would come inside any second now, but it sounded like Crick was in serious trouble!

When she heard another low, whimpering growl, all doubt was erased from her mind. Crick was definitely hurt!

Even if her mother had been right beside her, tying her securely to the kitchen door, Llyssaer would have fought. Her decision made, she turned and moved hastily down the hallway leading to the back bedrooms. She had to find her dog!

They walked through the cool, cloudy mist for a while in an odd, comfortable silence. Llyssaer held onto the back of Joy's shirt with a death grip while her mind raced through a menagerie of scattered memories revolving around her beloved, furry friend. Summer days filled with the repetitive throwing of a ball, Frisbee, or stick... he would fetch anything he could wrap his mouth around. If Crick could bite it, Llyssaer would throw it for him. When he was just a puppy, an innocent and energetic bundle of downy softness, he would follow her around the house for hours, always curious about what she was doing or where she was going.

At night, with a body still too small for his paws and a head which wobbled on his neck from its own weight, he would curl up in a makeshift bed, an opened cardboard box with one end cut off of it in a u-shape, but that didn't last long. As soon as he grew large enough to learn how to jump up on her bed, he slept at her feet, her everlasting knight in furry armor.

God, how she missed him! He had been her companion, her protector, her unconditional best friend. He had always been there for her every time she needed to talk about things that were bothering her. Even after he died, she couldn't help but talk to him as if he was still there, lying somewhere beside her on the floor. Even after he had died...

Although the mist swirling around her was cool and moist, she didn't feel it. Her eyes began to burn when hot tears pooled inside the lids while memories, both good and bad, rushed both around and through her like a storm-raged river. She squeezed her eyes closed, wanting to force the wetness away from her vision as much as needing to push those hateful, emotionally painful pieces from her past back into a dark, far away corner of her mind.

Joy still led the way, her shirt clenched in Llyssaer's tight grasp, taking them deeper into the forest. Joy stopped abruptly but Llyssaer didn't notice it in time because she was using her free hand to wipe tears away from her closed eyes. As a result, she bumped into Joy's back with a grunt and her eyes sprang open.

"Oh!" she squeaked in surprise. "Sorry."

Joy didn't seem to notice.

"We're here," the fair-haired girl said quietly as she took a small step forward.

Llyssaer used her free hand again to brush away a lingering pool of liquid from her left eye, embarrassed when she realized Joy would see the unmistakable, raw emotion all over her face. As she glanced at her new friend, Llyssaer was relieved to see that Joy was focused not on her sadness, but instead on something ahead of them.

Without a word, Joy moved to the side and Llyssaer released the blonde girl's shirt from her aching fist, and what she saw as she dropped her hand to her side caused her to forget about her embarrassment from just a few seconds before.

They were still standing well within a wide cluster of trees which was part of the woods they'd walked through to get here. Beyond the trees and just a few feet ahead of them, the path they had been following narrowed and spilled into an open valley of chartreuse colored grass and lumpy weeds. Scattered in no form or pattern throughout the yellow and green vegetation were hundreds, possibly even thousands, of headstones and grave markers. Almost all of these were partially covered with wide fingers of green moss, while others were completely coated with a thin film of the flowerless plant.

It was a giant cemetery.

Llyssaer had seen her share of graveyards in her lifetime. A particular one which came to mind was a very small, private burial place back in her old neighborhood and near the house she'd grown up in. Her curiosity about any possible new arrivals to the sacred site had brought her back to that old, miniature cemetery a few times a month when she was younger. Every time she'd been by to investigate, the gravestones had all been standing upright and, although she'd never seen any new ones there that she could remember, she couldn't help but run her fingers across the cold, mossy concrete slabs, tracing the names of those who called the uneven patch of hallowed ground concealed by a large swath of rhododendrons home.

Joy walked ahead while Llyssaer stood next to a tree whose trunk was painted with the invasive green moss, staring at the scenery. She raised her hand to her eyes and peered into the distance, unable to believe the number of gravestones scattered across the land. It was quite beautiful yet eerie at the same time. How many bodies rested beneath the surface of this quiet place? How many were friends, neighbors, or family members?

She smiled briefly as she thought about how a graveyard, especially one as large as this one, was just a giant cacophony of souls.

Joy had stopped just a few paces away and was waiting for her, but before Llyssaer followed, she noticed how much the atmosphere around them had condensed. The weather had changed quite a bit while she and Joy navigated their way through the thick stand of trees between the school and the cemetery.

With a glance overhead, she realized the sky had filled with gray clouds and a slight breeze had kicked up. *It looks as though it is going to rain soon*, Llys thought absently, but instead of worrying about the weather, she could only stand beside Joy and take in the scenery. Frozen in motionless wonder, she stared at the field of headstones dotting the rolling hills, spanning across the countryside almost as far as her eyes could see. Some of the concrete grave markers reached high into the fog while others huddled together, hugging the ground where they held tightly to their eternal owners. One of them, a tall, rectangular piece of aged and weathered chiseled granite, was leaning so far to the right that Llyssaer thought it might actually fall down on its side at any moment.

She took a slow, careful step forward; just far enough to take her away from the edge of the tree line and into the outskirts of the field. As if it suddenly found a life of its own, the fog from the forest suddenly thickened and expanded behind the girls, swirling in slow motion around tree trunks and across the countless leaves covering the ground. Llyssaer turned to ask Joy about the cemetery when she noticed the fog's shapeless arms as they began to envelope her. Before she had time to react, the misty swirls began at her feet and rapidly worked their way up her body. As the blanket of gray silently covered her face in a thick wall of chilly air, Llyssaer became frozen with fear.

She couldn't see! The fog had come to life behind them and, after covering her feet, swallowed her from bottom to top. The cold air surrounded her, prickling the hairs on her arms with endless strikes of electricity. In an instant, she was completely enveloped in it.

She couldn't move! She couldn't breathe! It was alive! It was in her nose, eyes, and ears; it was in her lungs! She tried to scream but couldn't. The air was thick and alive and it was strangling her.

Although she was nearly overcome with terror, a strange thought somehow broke through her senses. The air… smelled. It had a foul, burnt odor to it. Something… something, had burned. Something had burned horribly and the stench of it was nearly overpowering! It curled the hairs in her nose and made her eyes water. She choked as she tried to take a gulp of fresh air, but it was making her gag! She tried again to take a breath, but her throat had closed completely. She couldn't breathe!

She was going to die.

Llyssaer raised her hands to her neck, clawing at the sides as she struggled to inhale. She needed a long, deep breath of fresh air! Her lungs burned! Her hands burned! Her throat burned! She closed her eyes.

She was going to die.

Just when she thought she would never taste sweet, cool air ever again, her lungs abruptly filled. It was glorious!

Until she realized what the stench had been. It was hair; someone's hair was burning.

The distinct sound of a dog whimpering nearby brought Llyssaer back to reality. She was lying on her side on a cool, hard floor, but where? For several seconds she remained where she was, gasping for air. She couldn't breathe but she tried not to panic.

She remembered experiencing this same feeling a few years ago when she'd climbed, and subsequently fallen out of, a tree in Mrs. Ludwig's back yard. She'd lost her footing and slid down the trunk, landing on the ground with a thunderous thump. Conscious but disoriented, she immediately realized she couldn't take a breath. After the longest two minutes in her life, her lungs had finally begun to work again, but during that time, she'd been certain she was going to die.

What she was experiencing now felt just like that.

After her fall from the tree, her mother had explained, "If something like this ever happens to you again, even though it is thoroughly frightening, you should do your best to sit quietly for a moment or two and take slow, deep breaths."

Almost hearing her mother's voice, Llyssaer rolled onto her back and tried to follow her mother's suggestion. As she did, the cobwebs in her mind slowly dissipated. She was lying on Mrs. Gren's hallway floor in the dark. She remembered now that she had turned to run toward the back of the house but had tripped over something. When she'd fallen, she'd dropped her flashlight and the wind had been knocked out of her, which was why she couldn't breathe.

Llyssaer didn't know what she had tripped on that had caused her to fall and be in the predicament she was in now, but before she could do anything, she had to get her breath back. She sat up and leaned against the wall, taking first one then another slow, deep breath.

She was starting to feel a bit better when a weak, low whimpering noise floated toward her from somewhere down the dark hallway. It didn't take long for her to recognize that the sound had come from one of Mrs. Gren's two back bedrooms.

Llyssaer struggled to her feet. It would have to be enough. She had to find her dog.

"Crick!" she whispered in the unlit hallway. "Come here, boy!"

She heard a thump, then another, but there was no sign of her familiar bundle of fur. She heard a single low, weak growl, another yelp of pain that quickly subsided to whimpers, and, eventually, silence.

"Crick?" she called, louder this time, but only the sound of chirping crickets just outside the living room window answered her. She strained her ears in the eerie darkness for any sign that her beloved dog was making his way to her, but still he didn't come. The tiny hairs at the nape of her neck stood up on end and her arms were coated in goose flesh. In spite of the warning bells screaming in her head, she knew she didn't have a choice. She had to go find him!

Llyssaer had a fleeting thought about

her mother and wondered where she was, but her nearly overwhelming worry about her dog pushed it aside. She had to find Crick!

Finally able to breathe without struggling for air, she picked up her flashlight and turned it back on. Whispering her faithful dog's name, she headed down the hallway. When she reached the first bedroom, she carefully shined the light through the opened doorway, around the corner, behind the door, and under the bed. There was no sign of Crick. Eventually, she panned the flashlight beam across the room to the closed closet door.

Could he be inside?

Her head ached and her stomach was doing unmistakable flip flops from fear. With a shaking hand, Llyssaer reached out slowly and grasped the cold, round knob. She turned it silently and pulled the door open. Although she heard no sound coming from behind the closed, wooden panel, she couldn't help but anticipate her dog pouncing playfully through it and jumping onto the bed, like he did sometimes at their house. Instead, the only thing that greeted her as she pulled the door open was a thick, horizontal row of hung up sweaters and dresses on a rod, a cluster of neatly lined shoes across the floor, and the distinct scent of moth balls.

She quietly closed the door and headed back the way she had come. There was one more bedroom to check.

When Llyssaer returned to the hallway, she saw the door to the other bedroom was half open. She made her way toward it, quietly calling her dog's name.

"Crick? Crick-a-tick? Come here, boy."

In the distance she heard a siren and quietly wondered if it was coming this way. Had her mother reached the police department when she called? Llyssaer paused briefly and glanced down the hallway toward the kitchen, wondering again where her mother was.

A whimpering sound from the second bedroom drove all thoughts of anything except Crick from her mind. She had no doubt at all that the sound she'd just heard had come from him. Crick needed her!

"Crick?" she called out as she turned her attention back to the second bedroom and pushed the door open. Shining her flashlight through the doorway, she spotted a pair of hairy, back legs just beyond the far end of the bed. He was lying on the floor.

"Crick!" she cried.

Without any hesitation, she ran to her beloved pet and, as she made her way to his side, she heard him whimper again. She rounded the corner of the bed began to drop to her knees but stopped cold when she realized why he was lying down.

Both of his front legs were bent at unnatural, odd angles and his face was smeared with blood.

"Crick?" she whispered as she quickly dropped to the floor beside him. Hot tears of anger, sadness and confusion flooded her eyes. He raised his head weakly when he heard his name, and she felt his tail tickle her leg as he tried to wag it. "Crick, what happened to you?"

She moved the beam of her flashlight toward his head and gulped back a cry when she saw a puddle of blood soaking the carpet beneath it. The stain was getting larger with each second. She quickly got to her feet and said, "Don't move, boy! I'm going to get Mom."

As she turned to make her way back

toward the door, she was just about to yell, "Mom! Mom, come fast! Crick is hurt! He's bleeding, bad," but before she could say anything, the scene around her made her stop short and catch her breath in surprise.

The bedroom was a shambles. Normally, Mrs. Gren kept her rooms, every one of them, very neat and tidy. This was the older woman's bedroom and, after all the times Llyssaer had been here visiting, she'd never once seen it in the disarray it was in now.

Along one wall, the drawers from the long dresser were pulled out and clothes had been thrown in every direction. On top of the dresser was an antique jewelry box that Mrs. Gren's mother had given her years ago, rumored to have belonged to her great grandmother. One of the doors had been pulled off its hinges and the drawers within had been removed and lay in upturned piles on top of the dresser. Various pieces of jewelry were scattered around the ruined jewelry box like forgotten toys.

The bed, usually so well made that you could bounce a quarter on it (a result of Mrs. Gren being raised by a former Marine) was now a rough sea of sheets and blankets. The blue and red print comforter was hanging halfway down one side and partly on the carpet. When her eyes moved beyond the bed to the pillows that had been tossed haphazardly on the floor near the end of the dresser, Llyssaer's heart jumped into her throat.

A man stood in the corner, watching her. His face was smeared with black paint, perfectly matching his hair, shirt and pants. In one of his gloved hands he held a bloodied baseball bat. His wide eyes were dark and wild.

"All I wanted was a few pieces of jewelry and any hidden cash from that old coot," he hissed quietly. "That was all I wanted, but your dog, your *stinking* dog, had to come in and ruin it for me!"

He raised the bat with one hand and slapped the thicker end of it into the palm of the other. "A little bit of money, a little bit of jewelry, an old woman who would no longer need social security, and I woulda been outta here in a flash. But no! Your mangy mutt had to come in and screw up my plan!"

Llyssaer stood still, the beam of her flashlight shaking.

"Why did you hurt my dog? Why did you hurt Mrs. Gren? She never hurt anyone and neither did Crick!" she whispered as tears streamed down her face.

The man growled at her.

"Never hurt anyone?" he asked angrily. "What do you call this?"

He turned so Llyssaer could see the back of one of his legs. There was a gaping hole halfway between his knee and ankle and something was dangling from the outside of his pants. She turned the beam of her flashlight towards it and cringed when she realized what had happened.

His pant leg and part of his calf had been ripped open. Although she hadn't been able to make it out in the dark, she now realized that the material on the injured leg was soaked with the man's blood. The sneaker was black and glistened with moisture, and the carpet beneath his feet was stained with the sticky, red liquid.

"Your troublesome cur deserves what he got!" the man said angrily.

"No!" she said defiantly as anger replaced her fear. "You got what *you* deserved! You don't even belong here!"

"Llyssaer, where are you?" she heard her mother's voice suddenly from somewhere near the kitchen.

"I'm in the bedroom!" she yelled back, "and Crick is hurt bad! He needs help!"

Deciding to run into the hallway to get her mother, Llyssaer turned and bolted for the door.

Although he appeared to be seriously injured, the man in the corner moved fast. Realizing what she was about to do, he launched himself into the tall dresser which stood close the bedroom's entrance. With a thump and a grunt, the dresser fell away from him into the back of the door, pushing the thick panel of wood closed as it did so.

Llyssaer quickly understood what was happening but decided to go for it anyway. If she moved really fast, she could make it through the door before it closed. Then she could get her mother, and the police would come, and they would take Crick to the vet and get him fixed up and rush Mrs. Gren to the hospital. Before she knew it, they would be back at Mrs. Gren's table, telling jokes and eating chocolate chip cookies. They would…

But it was too late.

Just before Llyssaer reached the edge

of the door, it slammed shut. When she realized she wouldn't make it through the doorway in time, she tried to stop herself but couldn't. She bumped into the closed door as the dresser finished its fall. It landed on her like a giant sack of potatoes, knocking her to the ground. With a cry of pain, she dropped her flashlight and crumpled beneath the dresser. She was trapped where she had fallen, pinned to the floor like a thick wad of gum on the sole of a shoe.

"I deserve what I get, you say?" the man hissed from somewhere in the darkness over the dresser. "I think not, you sniveling brat!"

"It's okay," Joy said as she placed a cool hand on Llyssaer's arm.

When she opened her eyes, Llyssaer was still surrounded by a cloud of fog, although it was much thinner now than it had been seconds… minutes… hours before. It took her a few moments to recognize that she was on her knees in a thick patch of leaves with brown stalks of grass poking skyward here and there.

"What happened?" Llyssaer asked as she looked around, feeling as though she had just woken up from a bad, a very bad, dream.

"It's okay," Joy said again, holding out her hand to help Llyssaer get to her feet. "It's the natural progression. This is why you are here."

Llyssaer frowned at Joy as she brushed leaves from her hair.

"Did I faint?"

Joy shook her head, "No. You are remembering."

Llyssaer frowned and stared at the blonde girl, still somewhat uncertain about why she was here and what Joy wanted from her. And why did she talk in such riddles?

"I don't understand," Llyssaer said as crinkled lines of confusion created narrow valleys across the bridge of her nose. "That wasn't a memory. I must have been dreaming…"

"Come on," Joy said. With a reassuring smile, she turned and began moving into the field of gravestones. "We're almost there, but not quite. When we get where we're going, I'll help you understand, and so will Jiminy."

"I don't know if I should go any further," Llyssaer said hesitantly. She wasn't sure about what had just happened to her, but whatever it was it had left an uncomfortable feeling of dread throughout her entire being.

Joy ignored her companion's

uncertainty and continued leading the way up the hill into the sea of granite grave markers. When Llyssaer realized that this determined young girl wasn't going to stop, she turned to go back the way she had come. She'd only taken a few steps when a single sentence from the now familiar voice of the stranger she'd followed into the woods made her stop dead in her tracks.

"I understand you're scared and confused, Llys, but if you don't follow me now, you'll never know what happened to your beloved dog."

Llyssaer stood just a few steps away from the tree line, staring into the thinning fog as it swirled around the trees while she considered Joy's words. Although something inside her insisted she should return to the school, a larger part of her, her soul, perhaps, begged for her to follow the girl to the end. She wanted to know what was there; she *needed* to know.

"Llyssaer, I'll not force you to come with me, nor will I beg. All I can do is ask that you accompany me and promise that you will understand everything if you do. If you choose to go back to the school now, do as you must, but know you will never, ever, be given an opportunity like the one before you now to understand…

"Life is precious and it's unfortunate that so very few people understand this simple fact. So many take things for granted – the air they breathe, the food they eat, the sun that warms their skin, the water they drink. A large number of these same people never have a chance to understand life, or love, on a much grander level, but I'm offering this to you, my friend.

"Life is precious," Joy repeated, "and love is precious. Come with me, so you may really, truly see what I mean."

For several seconds, Llyssaer stood motionless within the shadows of the trees, listening to Joy's words as tears flowed freely down her face and questions swirled through her mind like a cyclone.

What was the bad dream she'd been having just a few minutes ago? What had happened to Jiminy and Mrs. Gren, and why on earth had she had such an evil and gory dream in the first place?

Jiminy had died. She knew this. But now, standing here on the edge of a wide, spacious cemetery in an unfamiliar place, Llyssaer suddenly couldn't remember how. Or why. What had happened to her dog?

She closed her eyes and tried to remember, but in her mind's eye all she could see was the man standing in the corner of Mrs. Gren's bedroom. Who was he and why had he hurt the sweet, gray-haired woman in her dream? Mrs. Gren had been their wonderful neighbor in Connecticut, and Llyssaer had left the grandmotherly woman as well as all of her friends behind when they'd moved to this strange, oh so strange town a few months ago. She loved both of her parents, very much, but she'd hated to move away from the place she'd called home for so long. Her parents assured her that they didn't have a choice. As a result, neither had she.

As for the blonde girl staring at her from the field of seemingly endless gravestones, Joy seemed innocent enough, but could she really be trusted? Llyssaer thought she could, but she couldn't deny that something very, very strange was going on.

"Make your choice, Llyssaer, for it is your choice to make. I know you can't say that about many decisions in your life, but this one, my friend, is yours and yours alone."

Joy paused as she considered her next words then offered a reassuring smile to the girl with the backpack.

"I will make my way to the place over there," Joy said as she pointed to the area where the cemetery crested the wide, green hill in the distance. "On the other side is a beautifully large oak tree. Not far from it is my destination. Follow me if you will. Or don't. If I reach the place on the other side of the hill and you have not followed, I will bother you no more."

Joy stared at Llyssaer for a long moment while the dark-haired girl considered her choices. A wave of emotion spilled across Llyssaer's face but, eventually, she made her decision. Without a word, she stepped forward and headed back into the cemetery.

Joy smiled at her and nodded.

"It will be okay, Llys. You will see."

After several seconds, Llyssaer reached the place where Joy was standing, but this time, instead of clenching the back of her shirt, the two girls walked slowly, side by side, and headed deeper into the field of mossy headstones.

Although the bank of fog from the woods still swirled around them and covered the landscape as far as the eye could see, it had suddenly begun evaporating. They walked through the cemetery, leaves crunching beneath their feet, and Llys was relieved that the misty blanket around them was dissipating. She didn't want their destination, whatever it was, to be hidden by swirling, smoky white fingers and unable to be viewed from a distance.

As she approached the top of the hill she could no longer deny the sudden, overwhelming urge to know what was on the other side.

She wanted, no *needed*, to see it; to understand it.

And she did.

When they crested the hill, Llyssaer stopped, amazed at the immense beauty before her.

About two hundred feet down the other side of the hill, where the grass was lush and green, stood a massive and thickly leaved oak tree. Its multitude of branches stretched upward, outward, and downward in a jointed maze of sticks and leaves, all reaching out for a hug. The entire tree must have spanned an area nearly as wide as her old house in Connecticut; it was absolutely gorgeous.

The trunk of the tree was wide and discolored, the wood littered with endless, winding wrinkles, courtesy of time, weather, and unseen insects. It looked as though the tree had called this side of the hill home for a very long time.

Not far away from the base of the tree stood a single large and fairly new headstone.

"It's lovely," Llyssaer whispered, her earlier bad dream long forgotten as she stared at the sprawling landscape. Although she found it a bit hard to believe, the cemetery on this side of the hill also stretched as far as the eye could see. Flowering bushes and a multitude of trees had been planted in various places among the gravestones throughout the entire cemetery, providing well-spaced as well as ample shade for anyone who might visit.

It was beautiful.

As she mentally questioned how far and wide the cemetery boundaries might go, Llyssaer found herself wondering what the name of the place was. She had only lived in this town a few months, but as far as she knew, no one had ever spoken of any cemeteries nearby. She turned to look at Joy, who was staring at the giant oak tree now, and asked, "Joy, what is the name of this cemetery?"

While Llyssaer waited for the blonde

girl to answer, she rotated herself in an arc in order to take in the full view from the top of the hill. It was breathtaking. When she completed her circle and was facing the large oak tree again, she thought she saw dark movement near the giant oak.

The fog had thickened slightly around the tree's base and smoky tendrils swirled in a wordless whisper around the roots and rolled their way toward the nearby gravestone. Llyssaer stared at the area close to the concrete grave marker where she'd thought she'd seen the movement when Joy finally answered her question.

"It's called Fate's Haven. It's appropriate, isn't it?"

Llys nodded while her gaze remained transfixed on the gray, wide slab marking the grave. Whatever the dark thing was that had moved near the tree, there was no sign of it now. Had someone or something been crouching behind the stone marking the grave? Had she seen part of someone's shoe? Although she couldn't be certain, she thought it had resembled some sort of out of place dark feather duster.

"Joy," she whispered, her voice alarmed and nervous, "I thought I saw something move behind that gravestone, the one closest to the big tree. I think someone, or something, might be hiding there."

"It's okay. I knew we weren't alone. I was waiting for you to realize it, which you couldn't have done until you were ready."

Llyssaer nodded, not really having heard her, and added, "Maybe it was a squirrel." But when she realized what the blonde girl had said, Llys turned and looked at her with a quizzical expression.

"Ready for what?"

Llyssaer had agreed to come with Joy to the place that would be their final destination, but now the blonde girl made it sound so… mysterious… that it was almost eerie.

"It's almost time," Joy said quietly as she took a step away from Llyssaer then turned to look at her.

Before she could question Joy's last statement, Llyssaer heard footsteps approaching from somewhere back the way they had come. When she turned to see who it was, her heart sank.

The man who had been monitoring the cafeteria as she scarfed down her earlier breakfast of champions was approaching them. Although he was alone, his face was stern and unsmiling.

"Crap!" she whispered as she suddenly wondered if this whole thing was just a ploy to get her in trouble with her parents. Sure, pick on the new girl!

Llyssaer stared at the approaching figure and decided she'd had about as much as her confused mind and heart could stand. When her mother found out she'd skipped school today, even if it was only for part of the day, she wouldn't like it, not one bit. With a sigh, all Llyssaer wanted to do right then was climb back into bed and wake up again. She was ready for a "do over," something she and her friends used to do a lot when they played together as small children.

"Llyssaer, meet Mr. Kardin. Mr. Kardin, this is Llyssaer," Joy said as the man reached the top of the hill.

Without a word, Mr. Kardin stopped and extended a hand in greeting. Llyssaer turned her look of confusion first to Joy, then back to the man standing before her with his hand outstretched.

"Huh?"

Although she was completely confused, Llyssaer didn't want to be rude, so she reached out and shook the monitor's hand. His grip was firm, his hand cool.

"I know I shouldn't be out here," Llyssaer began to explain in hopes of lessening her punishment, but a blur of movement near the line of trees where the cemetery ended interrupted her. Joe, the Johnson twin she'd seen in the hallway as she made her way outside through the side door of the school, was slowly ambling his way up the hill to join them. Behind him were dozens of kids she recognized from the school, even Mike and the other boy who had picked up the overturned chair in the lunchroom that morning.

Why was the whole school coming into the cemetery? Hadn't Joy explained when she met her that this was a secret place that not many knew about?

Llyssaer couldn't help but stare at the approaching group of teenagers and immediately noticed there were teachers mixed in with the throng of bodies. Yep, the entire school, including the *Principal*, was marching up the hill toward them.

When the two groups converged, the large group of students remained strangely quiet and formed a wide ring around the two girls and Mr. Kardin. Llyssaer watched in an uncomfortable silence as the line of bodies stretched from the top of the hill and down the other side, eventually forming a crude circle. Also included in its confines were the large oak tree and the nearby headstone.

Joy stepped back toward Llyssaer and took both of the nervous girl's hands in her own.

"Llyssaer, the time has come for me, for us, to share with you what you've been waiting for," Joy said, her voice calm and reassuring.

Llyssaer's hands were shaking as her eyes scanned across the surrounding group. When she finally turned back to Joy, she felt herself lost in the blonde girl's gaze. What was it about her eyes? They were so familiar, so very familiar. Why was that?

Joy's grip tightened just a bit and she asked, "Are you ready?"

As soon as the words were spoken, the sudden flash of a memory nearly knocked Llyssaer backwards. Strong arms grabbed her elbows to steady her as Joy continued to hold tightly onto her hands.

Llyssaer stared at Joy and an immense lump seized her throat. Her eyes examined every inch of Joy's face as raw emotion threatened to tear her heart open – again. She stared into the gray eyes with green flecks, the bridge of her nose, and yes, there was the scar in the center of her right eyebrow that she'd gotten from bumping her head on the sharp edge of the coffee table when she was three. She'd told Llyssaer the story one day over a fresh batch of chocolate chip cookies and a tall glass of cold milk.

"No," Llyssaer whispered quietly as she tried to pull her hands out of the blonde girl's grasp. "It can't be!"

In spite of Llyssaer's struggles, Joy held her friend's hands firmly within her own and nodded.

"It's okay, Llyssaer, this is what you need to go through. Remember I said you will find answers to your questions? Well, I meant it."

"I don't want to be here anymore," Llyssaer said as her tears of sadness, confusion and disbelief transformed into moist lines of anger and coursed their way down her cheeks in ragged, damp paths. She struggled harder in an attempt to break free of Joy's grip on her and failed to notice the area of the human circle behind her as it shifted toward the two girls, gently encouraging them to move closer to the tree.

"I want to go home!" Llyssaer cried out. "Let me go! I want to go home!"

Although she struggled with all her might, firm hands secured her arms while Joy refused to let go of her hands.

"Llyssaer, stop!" Joy said, but the girl with the backpack refused. She wriggled and kicked, trying to escape, as her fear and confusion threatened to take her past the point of no return.

"Llyssaer!" Joy shouted, but still the girl ignored her.

Llyssaer closed her eyes and prepared to scream at the top of her lungs when a single word crashed through the thick blanket of emotion that threatened to smother her beyond hope.

"JIMINY!"

The single word was spoken almost like a chant by the entire group. When she heard the name of her beloved pet echo through every cell of her brain as well as each chamber of her heart, Llyssaer stopped struggling, opened her eyes and released the breath she'd taken in to scream. Her red-rimmed eyes turned to look at Joy but the blonde girl wasn't looking at her. Llyssaer tasted the salty tears that had streamed down her cheeks just seconds before as she realized that Joy's attention had moved back to the giant oak tree.

The group waited patiently while Llyssaer fought to gain control of emotions. Eventually, she calmed down and her moist eyes scanned the crowd. As Joy finally let go of her hands, those gripping her arms released them as well. Although she now stood on her own, Llyssaer could sense that those standing behind her were still close in case she needed them.

She wiped her eyes and nose on her shirt as an unexpected vision filled her mind.

Jiminy, lying in a pool of blood next to Mrs. Gren's bed. His front legs shattered by a baseball bat, the life in his eyes dwindling away while she knelt beside him, stroking his fur. Her beloved Jiminy; her Crick-a-tick. He was the best friend she'd ever had. Where had he gone? Was he in dog heaven somewhere catching Frisbees, balls and sticks?

Llyssaer closed her eyes. That's what had happened! Although she hadn't been able to remember it earlier she was suddenly slammed with the realization that her beautiful Crick had been killed in the home invasion next door. Not realizing she was doing so, she raised a hand to her face and covered her mouth in shock. Her poor, poor dog! Crick had died in Mrs. Gren's bedroom, but she and the grandmotherly woman had gotten out of the house…

Hadn't they?

A home invasion was something she'd heard about, something that happened to "other" people, but it wasn't something that happened in your own neighborhood!

"Joy?" Llyssaer asked quietly, wiping at her eyes as fresh tears streamed down her cheeks. Now, finally, she clearly remembered the event that had stolen the life of her beloved pet. Like a fleeting glimpse of some faraway place from the window of a moving train, an unexpected still-life image flashed before her and stuck in her mind like sap on a pine tree. She wondered why she'd never really understood it before.

Joy nodded and gently patted her arm. "It's okay, Llyssaer. You kno⸱ almost everything now."

"But there's something else," Ll⸱ said as she dropped her hand an⸱

that her beautiful Crick had been killed in the home invasion next door. Not realizing she was doing so, she raised a hand to her face and covered her mouth in shock. Her poor, poor dog! Crick had died in Mrs. Gren's bedroom, but she and the grandmotherly woman had gotten out of the house…

Hadn't they?

A home invasion was something she'd heard about, something that happened to "other" people, but it wasn't something that happened in your own neighborhood!

"Joy?" Llyssaer asked quietly, wiping at her eyes as fresh tears streamed down her cheeks. Now, finally, she clearly remembered the event that had stolen the life of her beloved pet. Like a fleeting glimpse of some faraway place from the window of a moving train, an unexpected still-life image flashed before her and stuck in her mind like sap on a pine tree. She wondered why she'd never really understood it before.

Joy nodded and gently patted her arm. "It's okay, Llyssaer. You know almost everything now."

"But there's something else," Llyssaer said as she dropped her hand and stared straight into the blonde girl's piercing, gray eyes. "Are you related to Mrs. Gren? I think you are because I can totally see the resemblance in your face. In fact, it looks like you even have the same scar in your eyebrow that she had. Did you fall and bump your head on the coffee table, too?"

Joy didn't answer her. Instead, she offered a mysterious smile and turned her attention back to the oak tree.

Llyssaer followed Joy's gaze. This time she was certain she had seen something move behind the gravestone. She stood stock still, mesmerized, as the unidentified shape she'd caught sight of earlier finally emerged from behind the wide slab of granite. Once it was fully out in the open, the formerly hidden creature lay down on the hilly mound and stared at the group.

Silence enveloped them. As if on cue, even the wind was still.

Frozen in place, Llyssaer felt her heart pounding in her chest and her pulse raced through her veins. There was no way this was possible! She simply couldn't be seeing what she thought she saw! Her eyes *had* to be deceiving her! She couldn't move – all she could do was stare at the creature lying on the grass; its wide, brown eyes were just as she remembered. After what felt like an eternity, she raised a hand to her mouth to stifle a cry and her breath caught in her throat.

Consumed with disbelief, Llyssaer locked eyes with the creature for several long seconds then collapsed to her knees as fresh tears spilled down her cheeks. She couldn't believe this was real, yet she couldn't deny it. She was almost afraid to move, afraid to breathe, because it might make him go away. She slowly took a breath in, then out, but still he remained. Although he was watching her closely, he appeared to be waiting for something.

"Llyssaer," Joy said quietly, "I know you are overwhelmed, but there is one more thing you must do. In order to get the final answers to your questions, you must acknowledge him. That's it. Once you do that, the rest will fall into place."

Llyssaer didn't look at Joy because her eyes were locked on the form lying patiently on the mound of cool, green grass. She heard the words, though, and nodded her ascent with a sniffle. With hope filling every cell in her body, Llyssaer took a deep breath, placed her hands on her knees and leaned slightly forward. When she finally spoke, her words were barely a whisper, her tears clogging her throat as the words struggled to come out.

"Crrrrrk...." She paused, cleared her throat, and tried again. "Crick, come here boy."

As soon as the words were spoken, the dog rose to his feet and bounded to his mistress. Llyssaer held out her arms and he lunged into them, nearly knocking her over backwards. She was laughing and crying at the same time, holding him tightly against her body. He was warm and solid, and that familiar scent of him, the one she'd never thought she would ever experience again, filled her nostrils. She couldn't believe he was here. Her beautiful Jiminy, her Crick-a-tick! He was really here!

The crowd around them cheered loudly as they smiled and clapped with glee. They watched the girl and her dog for a short time then Joy knelt down beside Llyssaer and stroked the dog's full, glossy fur.

"Llyssaer, there's one last thing, and then that's it. I promise. It's more something you must know, not necessarily something you must do."

"It's okay, I know enough," Llyssaer answered abruptly while shaking her head. Changing the subject while scratching the Shepherd behind the ears, she added, "Isn't he beautiful? Oh, how I've missed you, boy!"

"Llyssaer," Joy said again as she placed a gentle hand on the ecstatic girl's arm, "you don't understand. There is still one more thing you must know, and you must see it must happen soon, or…"

Llyssaer interrupted her and said, "No, really, I don't need to. I'm happy with what I've learned. I have my buddy back! And actually, I think I need to get going. We really should go home. I know Mom won't be happy that I skipped school today, but when she sees Crick, she'll understand!"

She got to her feet, turned, and began walking back toward the line of trees at the far end of the cemetery. She slapped her thigh as she went, indicating to Jiminy that he should follow her, but Llyssaer had only taken a few steps through the circle of people at the top of the hill when she realized she was walking alone. This surprised her. In the past when she had called him like this Jiminy would happily bound past her in the direction she was going. But this time he hadn't. When she turned back to see what he was doing, she saw that the dog had made his way back over to the grass-covered grave where she'd first seen him.

"Crick? Come on, boy! Let's go home!" she called out, slapping her thigh again.

Still he didn't move. At first she thought maybe he hadn't heard her, but when he whined she somehow knew he had. He remained where he was, his sad, brown eyes reaching out to her across the field of grass covering the ground between them.

"Crick? What's wrong, boy?"

Joy shook her head. "He can't leave until you see the final part of your destiny, Llyssaer."

"I don't need to see...," Llyssaer began, but Joy raised a hand with a scowl of impatience. When the blonde girl spoke again, her tone was sterner than ever before.

"You don't understand, Llyssaer! He is running out of time. When he does, not *if*, which will vee

y soon, I'm afraid, he will leave. When that happens you will never see him again."

Llyssaer stared at Joy for several seconds then adamantly shook her head.

"Are you crazy? He's fine, don't you see? He's probably just hungry and really tired. I need to take him home…"

As she said this, Llyssaer turned and looked at Jiminy again. Just as she was about to order him, in a more harsh voice, to come with her, the words got tangled up in her throat. Instead of using a tone of authority, her words came out in a whispered croak.

"Crick? What's wrong, boy?"

Although the dog was still lying on top of the grave, his fur was no longer thick and glossy. In fact, he almost seemed to shimmer, as if he was in the process of fading away.

"Crick!" Llyssaer cried out, her wide eyes full of alarm.

"He won't be here much longer, Llyssaer," Joy warned as she took a step away from the girl beside her. "Go to him and see what he has to show you. Go, before it's too late."

Llyssaer wiped tears away from her eyes and slowly crept forward. She couldn't lose him, not again. If she did, she just didn't know what she would do.

She most certainly wouldn't want to live anymore.

Even though Crick had no sense of disrespect when it came to honoring the dead, Llys approached the grave with caution, careful not to step on the raised area. When she reached the dog, she fell to her knees beside him and reached out to stroke his fur, but instead of feeling the familiar, soft yet bristly texture of his coat, her hand slipped through him. In an instant, she recognized the crisp, green grass beneath him.

"Crick!" she shrieked, realizing that, although he was still lying next to her, peering up at her, he wasn't. She turned to Joy, her frantic eyes filled with panic. "What's happening? Joy? What's happening to him? Why can't I touch him?"

Joy didn't answer. Llyssaer stared at the blonde girl, waiting for her reply for several seconds when she realized that Joy wasn't looking at her at all. The girl who had been a complete stranger to her only that morning was focused on something behind her. In an instant, Llyssaer realized what it was – the gravestone.

When Llyssaer turned to look at the

thick slab of concrete, Crick-a-tick whined softly, as if from a distance. She was just about to call out for him again when the writing inscribed on the headstone told her all she needed to know.

Now she understood. Oh, God, did she understand.

"Llys, where are you?" her mother's voice called from somewhere beyond the closed bedroom door. In the distance, the sound of wailing sirens was closer now.

"I'm here," Llys said, fighting to breathe, "but I'm stuck!"

She struggled to free herself from beneath the dresser, but the heavy piece of furniture wouldn't budge; not at all. Her head ached and her left arm screamed with pain. Had she broken it?

She turned her head and tried to see what the intruder was doing but all she could see was the bottom of his pants and his shoes. Her flashlight had gone out when she dropped it but she could hear the darkly clad stranger moving around the bedroom. After several long seconds she heard a splashing sound. It didn't take long after that before a familiar scent found its way to her nose and her heart sank. It was gasoline.

Her eyes adjusted to the darkness and she could just see part of Crick across the room, lying in the same place she'd originally found him on the floor. He wasn't moving.

"Crick?" she called out as her eyes filled with tears again. Instead of hearing any sound from her beloved pet, she heard a chuckle from the man with the gasoline can.

"He's a goner," the stranger hissed triumphantly. "But then again, so are you."

The man came into view when he stood at the window on the far side of the room. He slid the glass upward, pushed the screen out into the yard and climbed through.

"See ya later, troublemaker," he said as he steadied himself on something outside. At first it looked as though he was going to simply walk away and Llyssaer began to think everything would be okay, but just before his body moved beyond the view of the window, it returned. The shadowed man leaned slightly back inside the gaping hole and his eyes shone bright with triumph. The baseball bat was now nowhere to be seen. Instead, in his right hand he held a match stick, and in his left, the box it came from.

"Llyssaer?" her mother called from the hallway just outside of the door. A hand banged on the other side of the door and the door handle turned wildly. "Honey, are you in there? Are you all right?"

"Mom! Mom, hurry! He's got a match! I'm stuck, and Crick isn't moving!" Llyssaer sobbed. She'd never been so afraid in her life.

A second later, any other words she might have had for her mother were sucked away by the giant vacuum which enveloped the room as the lit match landed on the bed and the entire room burst into flames.

She lifted a shaking hand to the cool slab of granite and traced the letters of the first name engraved upon it.

Llyssaer

The letters had been carved out of the stone beautifully, the font a stunning, flowing script. She'd always loved writing her name in cursive and she was glad they'd chosen to do it just this way.

She felt something cool nudge her arm and turned to see what it was. Crick-a-tick had regained his opacity and was once again touchable and vibrantly colored. He nuzzled her elbow and she wrapped her arms around him, digging her fingers deep into his fur.

Looking back at the headstone, she clearly read her full name, her date of birth, and her date of death. When she read the phrase below the dates, she couldn't help but smile.

Beloved Daughter

∾ and ∾

Lover of Nature

As the reality of what she was seeing sunk in, she plunged her face into Crick's fur and hugged him tightly, never wanting to let him go.

"Llys."

The adult voice was familiar but not one from those she'd seen standing around her in the cemetery. Although there was no doubt it was here with her now, it originated from her past.

She lifted her face out of Crick-a-tick's soft fur and slowly turned to acknowledge the owner of the voice. She didn't know how it could be so but she wasn't surprised to see the owner of that wonderful, beautiful, grandmotherly voice.

Mrs. Gren stood next to the giant oak tree, her gray hair short and perfectly in place. Everyone else was gone. Although the young, blonde girl was also nowhere to be seen, Mrs. Gren wore the familiar pink shirt with purple and yellow flowers, which fit her adult form perfectly. She held out her arms to Llyssaer, her eyes filled with love, understanding, and infinite patience. Without any hesitation, Llyssaer quickly rose to her feet and went to the woman.

Sobs of pain, sadness, love and relief racked her body like never before, and Mrs. Gren held the girl tightly until she had finished her tearful cleansing. When Llyssaer's sadness finally subsided, the gray-haired woman held out a handkerchief so the girl could blow her nose and, eventually, they sat down on the grass with their backs against the tree. They both somehow knew they weren't quite done yet.

Llyssaer blew her nose again, wiped at her eyes, and stared at Mrs. Gren while she gently stroked Crick's coat.

"I'm sure you have questions," Mrs. Gren said, "so go ahead and spill them. Ask me anything."

Llyssaer nodded and thought for a long moment, understanding most of it now but definitely wanting answers to a few things that were still bothering her.

"Well," she said as she bit her lip, "I'm assuming something but I know you've always said I shouldn't assume anything…"

"Yes," Mrs. Gren said with a smile and a nod, "go on."

"Well," Llyssaer paused for a moment as she stared across the field of gravestones, "we didn't make it, did we? You and I…"

Mrs. Gren shook her head.

"No, Love, we didn't make it. I died from my injuries in my living room before the ambulance got there, and you died in the fire that selfish punk set in my bedroom."

Llys nodded.

"And the stench of something burning… "

"Yes," the older woman nodded, "it was the wonderful aroma of hair burning in the fire."

"Mine," Llyssaer said, but it was a statement, not a question. As she tried to think of other questions, she suddenly remembered hearing her mother on the other side of the door and her eyes filled with panic.

"My mom!"

Her words echoed across the valley and Crick raised his head in alarm. Mrs. Gren reached out and gently stroked the dog's head.

"She's fine."

Llyssaer looked at her in stunned disbelief.

"She is?"

Mrs. Gren nodded. "The police arrived a few seconds after your mother began banging on the bedroom door. As soon as the officer realized there was a fire in the bedroom, he dragged your mother out of the house, kicking and screaming."

Llys nodded then frowned. "The guy who set the house on fire got away through the opened window. He said he was there to rob you but Crick ruined it for him."

Mrs. Gren chuckled and offered Llys a gentle hug. "He ruined it for himself, Love. He would have gotten away scot-free if he'd simply taken my jewelry and ran. Instead he had to mess me up then mess you up. It turns out that, as he began to walk away from the house after tossing the match onto the bed, he was stopped by the first officer's partner. He's going to jail for a long time."

Llyssaer pulled a long piece of grass out of the ground and began to chew on it as she tried to understand everything.

"I wonder why it took my mom so long to come into the house," she thought out loud. "We ran to your house together when we realized it was where Crick had gone. Once we got there, she stood outside to call 911 while I ran inside. She asked me to wait, but I couldn't. I just couldn't. After that, I don't remember seeing her go in the house at all…"

"That's because the guy who set the bedroom on fire had an accomplice," Mrs. Gren explained. "The other guy had gone out the back door to make sure the coast was clear and heard you and your mom when you ran up to the house. He knew his buddy was inside and figured the guy in the bedroom could easily take care of you, but he thought it was more important that he take care of your mom. He snuck up on her and hit her over the head with a piece of wood, knocking her out."

"He did?"

"Yes, but she didn't stay out for very long, thankfully."

"And she's okay?" Llyssaer asked with obvious doubt.

"Oh, yes," said Mrs. Gren. "She had a knot on her head for several days afterward, but she ended up just fine."

Llyssaer nodded with relief. After another long pause, she asked, "What happened to the accomplice?"

"You know that young man up the street? I think his name is Willy?"

Llyssaer nodded.

"Well, he was taking his nightly neighborhood stroll like he always did and heard the approaching sirens. I think he also heard you yelling in the bedroom, so he came up to my porch to investigate. That's when he saw the other guy getting ready to go back into the house through the kitchen door, after he'd knocked out your mom. The second guy saw Willy approaching and took off through the back yard, but, of course, Willy being who he is, he pursued the guy and caught up to him two blocks away. Willy kept the accomplice on the ground until the cops got there and took him into custody."

Llys nodded again then looked around with startled eyes when she realized they were completely alone.

"Where did everyone go?" she asked. All of her fellow students and teachers, even Mr. Kardin, had disappeared.

Mrs. Gren smiled and stared up at the sky. The fog had lifted and a sea of deep blue now hovered far above their heads.

"You really don't know?" the gray-haired woman asked in a teasing tone.

Llys shook her head. "I really don't. Did they go back to school? Are they going to call my mom?"

As soon as her questions ceased, she realized how silly the last one had been. Of course they weren't going to call her mom because she must already know her daughter was dead.

"Okay, so forget my last question," Llyssaer said with a frown of embarrassment, "but seriously, where did the others go?"

Mrs. Gren chuckled again.

"Don't you see, Love? They're all dead. The school is to continue the education of those no longer living, and this cemetery is where they live; where *we* live."

Llyssaer thought about this for several minutes, then asked, "So, after these guys broke into your home and I…" she paused, struggling to say the word but eventually continued, "…died, I never moved away, did I?"

Mrs. Gren shook her head.

"In a way you did, but not really. Your parents moved to a place in Virginia, but you… your spirit went with them, but the physical you didn't. Everything you have experienced since the tragedy has been on a different level than what you'd known before. Before the tragedy you had life. Now you have a dream life."

The reality of the day's events finally sank in. This was her new home. She would stay here with Crick and Mrs. Gren.

"You're staying, too?" she asked, her voice shaking with sudden doubt.

Mrs. Gren nodded.

"I'm not going anywhere, Love."

"And my mom and dad, are you sure they are okay?"

The gray-haired woman hugged her and nodded again.

"They are. They miss you, and Crick, of course, but they are doing okay."

Llyssaer nodded and closed her eyes. She was tired after such an exhausting day.

"I think I'll take a nap," she said with a smile of relief. She gave Crick a scratch behind the ears and stretched out on the grass in the shade of the giant oak tree.

Mrs. Gren stood up and said, "Very good, Love. I won't be far away. When you wake up, I'll show you around."

"Okay," Llyssaer said with a yawn then lay her head down close to Crick.

"Sweet dreams," Mrs. Gren whispered.